SCOTTISH LEGENDS

Edited By Sarah Washer

First published in Great Britain in 2017 by:

Coltsfoot Drive
Peterborough
PE2 9BF
Telephone: 01733 890066
Website: www.youngwriters.co.uk

FOREWORD

Welcome, Reader, to 'Crazy Creatures – Scottish Legends'.

For Young Writers' latest mini saga competition, we asked our writers to dig deep into their imagination and write a 100-word story with a beginning, middle and end, about a unique and original crazy creature; and the crazier the better!

The result is this collection of fantastic fiction with wild and whacky creations! Prepare for an adventure as you discover different dimensions with amazing alien life, mad mashed-up monster battles, cool superhero quests, and why not befriend a fuzzy loveable beast? From the weird to the wonderful, there is something to suit everyone here.

There was a great response to this competition which is always nice to see, and the standard of entries was excellent, therefore I'd like to thank everyone who entered.

I hope you enjoy reading these stories as much as I did.

Keep writing,

Sarah Washer

CONTENTS

Ramsay Rostock (9)	55
Louie Macleod (8)	56
Will Russell (9)	57
Ellie Robb (9)	58
George Hannah (9)	59
Kaan Baran (9)	60
Riley Wilkinson (9)	61
Shayne Thomas (9)	62
Jack Mackie (8)	63
Lewis Alan Austin (9)	64

Riverside Primary School, Stirling

Iris-Mae Quilliam (9)	65
Brooke Mirren Tait (9)	66
Sonny Williamson Frame (10)	67
Stella Jamieson (9)	68
Olivia Miller (9)	69
Jack Connelly (9)	70
Phoebe Rose Saunders (9)	71
Jodie McDonald (11)	72
Jonah Braccio Bracciali (9)	73
Elizabeth Newby (9)	74
Poppy-Ann Poole (10)	75
Summer Maclean (11)	76
Farah Waddell (9)	77
Ollie Mawby (9)	78
Lucy Abigail Cameron (8)	79
Andrew Craig (9)	80
Samuel Vargovsky (11)	81
Evan Ross Gillies (9)	82
Kiara Steven (10)	83
Jennifer Raiston (9)	84
Robyn Elizabeth Harley (9)	85
Lillian Baxter (9)	86
Conal Doherty (11)	87
Joe Underwood (10)	88
Rushmail Afzal (9)	89
Eva Willow Coulter (8)	90
Anna Maria Blazejczyk (9)	91
Sophie Mulvenna (9)	92
Rhona Joanne Waldron (9)	93
Hekaya Makafui Esi Ry-Kottoh (10)	94

Lyla Campbell (10)	95
Nicole Elise Schiavone (9)	96
James Anderson Taylor (9)	97
Brian Duguid (11)	98
Rebecca Menzies (9)	99
Maya Templeton (8)	100
Callum Stephen James Dewar (10)	101
Zachary Ferguson (9)	102
Lewis David Paterson (10)	103
Emily Collington (10)	104
Sophie O'Sullivan (9)	105
Thomas Edmiston (9)	106
Gwen McAviney (11)	107
Mikolaj Jasinski (9)	108
Nuala Scully (10)	109
Callum Draper (9)	110
Abbie Coutts (8)	111
Ezra Jump (11)	112
Lewis John Reid (11)	113
Evan Rands (9)	114
Holly Matheson (10)	115
Connor Iain James Cadger (10)	116
Alex Harrower (9)	117

Stanley Primary School, Perth

Anna Brown (9)	118
Edward Trevallion (9)	119
Josh Jerome (10)	120
Cara Lee (10)	121
Olivia Keenan (9)	122
Dreanna Norris (10)	123
Ethan Sam Low (9)	124
Daisy Morgan (9)	125
Dillon Williamson (9)	126
Courtney Nicoll (10)	127
Alex Russell (9)	128
Ryan Andrew (9)	129

Tulloch Primary School, Perth

Jack Stephen (9)	130
McKenzie William Yeaman (10)	131

THE STORIES

Adventures

One day, a little girl was drawing a picture of a pink fluffy puffy monster. Suddenly, the monster came to life. 'Poof, puff, lala, wuff.'
'Hi, I'm going to take you on an adventure.'
Then a pink light came, *whizzeewooo*, which transported them to the jungle. Then they saw a big lion sitting on a medium-sized rock and lots of hippos swimming. They heard an 'oooo, ah, ah'.
The monkeys wanted them to swing on the vines. They started swinging, 'Wheee!' *Plop*, they fell down. 'Ouch!'
The girl was sitting in her bedroom, a tuft of pink fluff floated by...

Jessica Barnett (9)
Buchlyvie Primary School, Stirling

The Amazingly Short Adventure Of Sam The Shape-Shifter

Adrenaline pumped through Sam's purple veins as he transformed into Kevlar to protect him from the harsh atmosphere. A glowing chalk sphere hung in the sky, so Sam concentrated all his Bblutonian power into going completely invisible. Looking around him, people wore strange clothes. Worried he might be discovered, Sam shifted his molecular structure into an 'Earthling'. He turned and saw a massive vehicle heading straight for him. Quick as a flash, Sam turned into liquid and let the vehicle run over him. *This place is way too intense*, he thought. *I'm going home!*

Bryce Henley-King (11)
Buchlyvie Primary School, Stirling

Crash-Landing!

Crash! Bang! Snap! 'Breaking news, a spaceship has just crash-landed on Earth!' said Eamonn Holmes on the news.

'Who is in it?' cried the townspeople. Only one person, or should I say monster, knew who it was. It was Flumfledumple (or Flumfle for short). Flumfle was wriggly and bumpy, he had talons as sharp as needles. Flumfle also had an extraordinary head shaped like a star. Well, it was ordinary on his home planet, Zargafrase. Earlier, Flumfle had called for help but got a humongous shock when his arch-enemy stepped out of the spaceship... Momojeje!

Murrin Thomson (10)
Buchlyvie Primary School, Stirling

Lost In Space!

Look over there, Jawrawsaw is eating blue pizza, an orange milkshake and a tub of grey ice cream. Sure it is weird how Jawrawsaw gets his food from the river, something like 100 yards away. Suddenly, a policeman storms through the door like a bull. It looks like he is about to shoot Jawrawsaw. 'Uh-oh,' he says, 'I'm about to go into space!'
'OK,' says the officer. Then Jawrawsaw gets into his rocket and goes into space. He sees a sign that says 'Pluto' with an arrow pointing north. Then Jawrawsaw shouts very loud, 'I'm lost!'

John Winther (7)
Buchlyvie Primary School, Stirling

Adventure Of Luus Stuul (Pronounced Loos Stool)

Luus Stuul was hiding from his mum and then suddenly a giant toilet flush crashed down on Uranus; all Luus Stuul saw was two brown blobs washing away... 'I will get my revenge!' shouted Luus Stuul, 'No matter how far I have to run! I must find the po'uo missiles because this time the toilet flushes have gone too far!'

'Yes, Commander Stuul!'

'Launching the po'uo, sir.'

'Well done, Lieutenant Plap.'

'Yay, the toilet flushes have stopped!' cheered Luus.

'Hooray, yeah, let's celebrate!'

Elis Williams (10)

Buchlyvie Primary School, Stirling

Zadork And Dasie

Zadork was a really scary creature who only had... well, no one! He only had enemies who were humans. One day he said, 'Go away, stupid humans.' But the humans started shooting at his planet, Jabor. They were trying to make his planet no more. Zadork went up to the humans and said, 'Please stop,' but they didn't listen. He was about to give up when Dasie, a girl, said, 'Stop please, this is his home, stop destroying it!' Luckily, the humans stopped and went home, and everyone lived happily ever after all together, for ever and ever.

Zoe Neil (10)
Buchlyvie Primary School, Stirling

The Deadly Blueberries

Benny was having fun rolling in the pool when suddenly, the wind blew him out. He crashed into a sunbed. Benny wanted to go somewhere. He started walking but he began to get tired and he was so desperate to stop. Benny looked in front and saw a beautiful ocean view. He went down the stairs, 'Aah!' he screamed in happiness. Suddenly, humans saw Benny and because he was red, round and squishy, people started throwing blueberries and he was falling over, trying to dodge the deadly blueberries. He got away and started walking again. He looked up...

Ruby Baker (10)
Buchlyvie Primary School, Stirling

Go Big Or Go Home

Aaron is a special type of monster, he's a Fluffymon and his aim is to win Olympic gold on the hoverboard in Moscow, Russia. Aaron is orange and blue, he's 123 years old, which for Fluffymon is quite young! Aaron is waiting in the back for his name to be called. He can barely move on his hoverboard as he feels so nervous. His name is called, Aaron takes his mark.

'...Mark, set, go!' *Bang!* Aaron takes the lead, chased quickly by second place. Aaron can see the finish line. Aaron wins gold! Aaron has done it!

Josh Stevenson (11)
Buchlyvie Primary School, Stirling

Globby Land

Globby likes to smash stuff. He smashes houses, cars, helicopters and planes. One day, something bad happened. Globby got out of control. Globby does this a lot but this time was different; aliens came from outer space and helped the humans. Globby was wondering when they were going to help him but the aliens didn't, so Globby smashed the aliens and their spaceships. Globby kept one spaceship but was so forgetful he forgot where he had hidden it. But in no time at all he found the spaceship and Globby got up to space, and got back to Globby Land.

Struan Ferguson (10)
Buchlyvie Primary School, Stirling

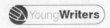

Chuck Saves The Day

Chuck climbs up out of his grave, ready to save the world from some giant beasts! He knows if he can get the humans' attention he can make an army to attack the giants. A few days later... the city is being roamed by giants as the humans helplessly fight but Chuck gives it his all. His eye laser is lethal against them. Finally, there's a duel between Chuck and Bloodthirsty, the evil leader. It is a tough fight but in the end everyone is cheering, 'Chuck! Chuck! Hip, hip, hooray! Hip, hip, hooray! Chuck, you're so cool!'

Reuben Brown (8)
Buchlyvie Primary School, Stirling

Eden In The Grass Realm

As Eden was slinking in-between the trees, her twenty eyes looked around. There it was, the Grass Realm. Her brown skin tingled as she turned green. The portal glimmered as she stepped through. The Grass Army was waiting for Eden when she was through. They pounced... Eden woke up with a Grass Creature guarding her. She screwed up her eyes and turned into grass. The guard yelped and undid the chains to check whether she was there. Eden ran, like she never had before, all the way into the forest. Eden turned into a tree and stayed forever.

Lily Winther (10)
Buchlyvie Primary School, Stirling

The One Who Lost It All

Blobby is a multicoloured blob who comes from the undiscovered planet called Blobland. His family are poor, his whole family grew up on the streets. His mum and dad had died because of an evil man called Shopzen. Shopzen had killed his parents and also taken the Spirit Stick, and Blobby wanted the stick back. One day, Blobby went looking for Shopzen but Shopzen captured Blobby and questioned him about where he lives. Blobby told him, got out of the rope, got the Spirit Stick and went home. But where is Shopzen now?
'Help!'

Sam Smyth (10)
Buchlyvie Primary School, Stirling

Bubbly Bubbles' Adventure

Bubbles is a rag doll cat that is brown and white. He has big, wide ears with rabbit-like paws and has multiple sizes of teeth. Some are sharp, pointed teeth like fangs. Bubbles is from Great Britain, his power is that he can point his paw and bubbles come out. He absolutely hates peopie. Bubbles was on his way to a sleepover, but on his way he met Peopie. Bubbles thought that Peopie would try to attack him but they didn't and Bubbles carried on, but he took a wrong turn and ended up in the really, really dirty water...

Sophie Armour (11)
Buchlyvie Primary School, Stirling

Untitled

One day, there was a girl called Pink-Sky but she was not any old girl. She had five eyes, six legs and hot pink skin. Yep, you guessed it: she was a monster, a friendly monster. She had some good tricks, she could take her legs off then grow them back and fly unexpectedly.

One day, she attended a party and floated away into the blue sky, through the clouds. All of a sudden, a big, fat, green cloud monster tried to attack. Luckily, she was a black belt in Ninja School. She dodged all his moves and killed him.

Kerri Skinner (10)
Buchlyvie Primary School, Stirling

The Adventures Of Poepie

Poepie was zooming past so speedily, the fish turned a full 360 degrees and started to swim backwards. The flash of blue and turquoise stopped and all the fish got a good look at him. Poepie had blue and turquoise stripes, one beady eye, a snake-like body with a fish tail, sharp jagged teeth and patches of wires on his body. He looked around, which way should he go? Suddenly, he got ambushed by Candy. Poepie shot at Candy with his super scales. Candy swam away and Poepie went on with his merry way. He never saw Candy again.

Jamie Donnachie (10)
Buchlyvie Primary School, Stirling

Crash Of The Aircraft

Jack Wilder somehow lands on a beach in Texas, then the next day there is an aeroplane crash. Conjour gets out of the crash then finds a bow and arrow, but it is not just any bow and arrow, it is Jack Wilder's. Jack Wilder is from Popalleypop where he does his magic tricks, but they aren't any ordinary tricks because he made the Tower of London disappear. Then the fight begins. Jack Wilder uses his signature move which is a back hand slap and Conjour faints, and Jack gets the bow and arrow and runs away.

David Adam (9)
Buchlyvie Primary School, Stirling

Alit The Lion Thing

One day, there was a little boy called Jack sitting in his bedroom. All of a sudden, a portal flew out of the ground. It started to pull everything into it. Jack got pulled into the portal and hit his head on something. He woke up in a rocky terrain, strange noises echoed through the terrain, bouncing off the rocks. All of a sudden, a 'miaow' came from behind the rock. A lion-type thing jumped up. Jack picked up a rock, he threw it at the four-eyed creature. The portal burst open again. Jack woke up in bed!

Archie McFadzean (10)

Buchlyvie Primary School, Stirling

Cubee And The Lost And Found

Cubee was a cube with a plant for eyes and cubes for feet. One day, he went to school and he lost his very special teddy. Cubee went to the lost and found and he found his teddy, but unfortunately on the way back to class he met his foe, Circlee. Circlee scared Cubee by jumping out from behind a tree so Cubee decided to turn Circlee into a frog with his magic powers. Cubee returned to class with his teddy and had a nice day. Circlee stayed a frog forever! Don't mess with Cubee, you may become a frog!

Erin McGee (10)
Buchlyvie Primary School, Stirling

Candy's Life So Far

In the part of Candy Land with the most candy, a baby bat-cat girl was born. She had a name, Candy. Candy had purple hair, bat ears and cat eyes, she also had dagger-sharp teeth. Ten years later, she was enemies with people and had murdered Bob the butler and Kevin the cook. Candy's mom and dad were raging, they sent her to boarding school. She went on a school trip and got so excited she turned into a bat. After that, she got suspended from boarding school. Candy went home and was locked in her room...

Freya Whitehouse Middleton (10)
Buchlyvie Primary School, Stirling

A Sticky Situation!

Eagle Eye flew through the sky, the wind blowing through his white feathers. Suddenly, he flew into a tree. *That is strange*, thought Eagle Eye as he patted the big red bump on top of his head. 'I know every single tree here and I have never seen this tree before.' Eagle Eye tried to get up but he seemed to be stuck to the tree! He took a closer look at this strange tree and noticed it was covered in small sticky pads. 'Stick Bot!' shouted Eagle Eye, 'I will get you next time!'

Bethan Henley-King (9)
Buchlyvie Primary School, Stirling

Monster School

Long Heed is a monster, a rare monster. He has the gift of being a cowboy but that's not all, he has a very long neck and three mouths. He also has two banana guns that shoot bananas, a pen as a knife and an apple which he can throw at his enemies. His best power is turning into a bat! Long Heed had been told to go to Planet Earth on holiday. When he arrived he started causing problems. He was in the classroom taking pencils then a bell rang, *drrriiinnngg!* and children came in and saw him...

Jack Brown (10)
Buchlyvie Primary School, Stirling

The Making Of Giblet Jaws

There was an evil man called Evil Doc Gustav and he created this creature that was 25% rooster, 25% duck, 25% monkey and 25% who knows what! His name was Giblet Jaws, he lived in Castle Vania and he had a supersonic sound. He can climb the tallest trees and he can swim in any sea, but all Giblet Jaws wanted to do was meet friends and not fight battles for Evil Doc. So he packed his bags and left Vania for Neverland, so he could help Peter Pan fight Captain Hook, and help Peter, Wendy and Michael get home.

Sophie O'Dell (9)
Buchlyvie Primary School, Stirling

22

The Moon

'Hi, my name is Star. My favourite thing is rainbows.' She was so cute and furry. One day, Star was walking on the moon and Star made a new friend called Rainbow. They jumped about until they saw a big destroyer called Cookie. It was 5cm tall. Then they blasted back home and ran all the way. Cookie went and destroyed the city! Star said to Rainbow, 'I hate destroyers, do you know my secret?'

'No,' said Rainbow.

'It is that I turn invisible.'

'Cool!' said Rainbow, 'Do you know my secret?'

'No.'

'I turn into a volcano...'

Emma Louise Green (10)
Caskieberran Primary School, Glenrothes

The Story Of Gruff

One extra creepy morning, Gruff woke up in a strange place. He thought, *This can't be Mount Syberia.* While Gruff was thinking, he caught lightning in his horns and saw a strange thing, magic. So he flew as fast as lightning up to the roof and he said, 'What is this strange creature?' in a heavy, deep voice. The creature flew down and everyone started screaming except for one, and that one said, 'Hi.'

Gruff flew out the window and said, 'OMG, this is so not Mount Syberia.' Then he saw a mountain so he flew over...

Chelsea-Leigh Lambie (10)
Caskieberran Primary School, Glenrothes

24

Rose Gets Caught

One Friday, Rose was bored because all her friends were away since it was Christmas break. Rose wasn't going on holiday, she normally goes in October. Her family didn't have a lot of money so she made her own fun. One thing her parents didn't know was that she had fireworks and rainbow potions in the attic. So she went outside and set the fireworks off. The problem was she couldn't get caught by humans. Rose forgot about the humans, she went to play with the fireworks and rainbows. As soon as she jumped out, a little girl saw her...

Erin Buddie (10)
Caskieberran Primary School, Glenrothes

The Devil's Child Day

There was a devil and his child called Devil's Child. Devil's days of mischief were over but Devil's Child was a mischief machine, always causing havoc. On Monday he made a prank, putting fake blood and a knife into crates. His teacher got such a fright she jumped right through the roof! He got in big trouble for that and for the rest of the week he did the same. His dad didn't approve of this, he really didn't approve, so Devil's Child followed in his dad's footsteps. Before he knew it, he was a prank-free devil.

Kian Laing (10)
Caskieberran Primary School, Glenrothes

The Undead

One day, on May 31st 1970, Joey was looking for people to eat. He looked in the jungle, on islands and on streets. He looked everywhere! Then suddenly there was a thud, a huge thud! It was a ginormous, giant, crazy monster. This monster was Joey's enemy, his name was Deathwater. He tried to catch Joey so he ran away as fast as he could. Deathwater had blood dripping down from his mouth, he looked scarier than Joey. He finally stopped chasing him. After he stopped chasing, Joey went to a place to look at fire and volcanoes.

Zoe Louise Findlay (10)
Caskieberran Primary School, Glenrothes

Furious The Fury

Furious the Fury is a pencil-stealing monster. He can turn invisible and sneak into the classrooms and steal all the pencils. One day, Furious the Fury was halfway through stealing pencils when his enemy, the Peaceonions from Planet Peace, came and tried to stop him from stealing pencils. All planets came to peace, everyone except Furious the Fury who still steals pencils. So if I were you I would keep a tight grip on your pencil or someday he could come to your classroom and steal your favourite pencil!

Jessica Brown (10)
Caskieberran Primary School, Glenrothes

Spikey's Worst Day

Spikey was on the sun but he was hungry so he was going to jump to Earth to get some food. Suddenly, he saw aliens so he had to shape-shift into an alien spaceship, but they came closer. When they got to Spikey, they asked, 'What are you doing here? We are going to Mars.'
Spikey said, 'I'll be there in a minute,' but Spikey didn't, he went to Earth and shape-shifted into a human, stole some food then jumped back to the sun. He ate his food and drank juice.

Brandon Lee (10)
Caskieberran Primary School, Glenrothes

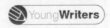

Death Blade's History

It was ten years ago when an evil monster called Kiki stole the legendary magical sword of Death Land. The sword is what keeps the balance to Death Land. Soon after the sword was stolen, Death Land started to crumble, but a brave girl went after Kiki and made it her mission to get it back. It took three long hard weeks but she got the sword back and saved her planet. The girl who is now a woman is called Harmony. She is now the keeper of the legendary sword Death Blade.

Katie Paul (9)
Caskieberran Primary School, Glenrothes

Joe The Volcano Guy

One day, there was a monster called One Eye Joe. He had no friends, no mum and he was alone. A school went to see a volcano and a small boy found One Eye Joe and took him home. He was scared! One Eye Joe liked his new owner. The boy found out that he was real and not a toy, and he was scared. The boy went to his mum then his mum chucked him out the door! One Eye Joe said that kids were his enemies. When he gets hungry, he gets kids and drinks their blood!

Isla Yule (9)
Caskieberran Primary School, Glenrothes

Fuzzy McFuzder's Adventure

One day, a little monster named Fuzzy McFuzder went shape-shifting. After all that shape-shifting, Fuzzy decided to go home, to a nasty surprise! All of his enemies were destroying his house. He ran off crying and he decided to move. He found a little village called Fuzington Village and so he lived there. Then the enemies found him and they started to sneak around his house...

Mia Osborne (10)

Caskieberran Primary School, Glenrothes

Mucky Mike

Ever wondered why the pencils keep disappearing and you keep getting the blame? Mucky Mike is the one who keeps stealing them and putting them in hard-to-reach places. He isn't a fan of assistant teachers because they keep getting new pencils out of nowhere. Mucky Mike hides the pencils so that the children can't do their work. If he gets close to getting caught, he uses his super speed to run away. So every time your teacher gets mad about disappearing pencils, blame Mucky Mike!

Craig Rankin (11)
Dalmally Primary School, Dalmally

Jelly Monster Attack

One day, there was a monster. His belly was made of jelly. The rest of him was not made from jelly. One day he went to school and when he got there, he was different from all the other children. They ran after him, he ran and ran then set a bomb off in his belly. All the jelly went everywhere! The children started eating the jelly. Then the monster was tiny, he was scared of everything and ran away from everybody. Then he was looking for jelly and found some, then he had a jelly belly back!

Tina Bell (10)
Dalmally Primary School, Dalmally

The Day Destroyer Became Angry

One day, Destroyer was minding his own business when a space robot came spying on him from around a boulder. He got so angry he turned into a monster with laser beam eyes. Destroyer burnt the robot to shreds and headed towards Earth. When he arrived at Earth, he started burning everything: houses, shops, cars, trains and planes. In about four hours he had burnt everything in the entire world. When Destroyer finished, he told all the other monsters on Mars to live on Earth.

Jake Campbell (11)
Dalmally Primary School, Dalmally

Eyetastic

Eyetastic went out of his test lab as all he could hear were the pigeons playing on his high rope. They always left a terrible mess! Eyetastic decided with his 17 eyes to keep lookout and wait for them so he could scare them away. They arrived on the high rope, Eyetastic shook the wire till they all flew away.

Ruaraidh Rankin (9)

Dalmally Primary School, Dalmally

Christmas Holidays

It's Friday morning and Prickle goes into school. It's the last day and that means Christmas! Prickle runs up to his friends, they all start talking about Christmas and what they want. That's the bell for lunchtime. Prickle starts talking... 'What, a new person?' Prickle goes over to the new girl. 'What's your name?' asks Prickle.

'Sesame,' says the girl.

'Would you like to come to lunch with me?'

'Yes please,' says Sesame.

'What do you have for lunch?'

'Cheese. What do you have?'

'Ham. Let's go outside.'

There's the bell for home time.

'See you soon, Sesame.'

'You too.'

Elizabeth Johnstone (8)
Hilton Of Cadboll Primary School, Tain

Shadow's Explosion

Shadow hates Earth so she has a plan. Shadow looked at herself in the mirror, she saw her amazing black ninja costume and looked at her shiny silver katana. Obviously she took a selfie! 'It is time,' she whispered as she flew down to Earth. When she got down she set off to get some TNT, only at nightfall. 'At last,' whispered Shadow, 'I've got all the TNT I need.' Shadow silently set up some TNT and she almost got caught. 'He he,' shouted Shadow as she pushed the lever and flew away.

'Huh?' shouted a human... *Boom, boom, boom!*

Aimee Campbell (9)
Hilton Of Cadboll Primary School, Tain

The Monster Who Meets The Grinch

The big slimy dragon slug called Masletrococoatap that lived on Planet Coctamoontracocoa decided she wanted to go to a different planet. So she came to Planet Earth and she was rather hungry, but all the takeaway and sit-in shops were closed. So she broke into a shop and ate all the food. In the morning she went to Mount Crumpit and met a teacher from Hilton Of Cadboll Primary School and ate the teacher. Masletrococoatap met the Grinch. The Grinch said, 'Do you want to help me ruin Christmas?' So Masletrococoatap said, 'Yes, of course I do!'

Eva Mcneill (9)
Hilton Of Cadboll Primary School, Tain

Eyeleg And Her Enemy, Bob

Once upon a spaceship, Eyeleg, a bright red creature, flew down from Planet Gladdop. Then something went wrong with the spaceship. Down, down, down it went, falling to a planet called Earth. Eyeleg got out of her spaceship to explore and found herself in Bob's mansion. Suddenly, she heard running, it was Bob. Eyeleg tried to turn invisible but Bob had seen her and started chasing her. Then she turned invisible so Bob tried to find her. He looked all around the house but it was too late because Eyeleg flew back to Planet Gladdop...

Madison Fleming (9)

Hilton Of Cadboll Primary School, Tain

Nearly Getting Killed

Hello, my name is Pinkoo. I'm from Hair Planet. I think I'm going to be attacked... Argh! I'm too pretty to die! Argh! OK, I am going to Earth.
'I don't care if you follow me, Homeworkgirl.'
'Well of course I'm going to follow,' said Homeworkgirl.
OK, let's get back to me. I love to take screenshots, I love the colour pink. I love to do gymnastics, it is life. I love to watch YouTube and I have a YouTube channel. But this is an annoying thing, my phone is stuck to my hand!

Freya Lewis (9)
Hilton Of Cadboll Primary School, Tain

Prodinosaur's World

Once, in a dark cave, there was a dinosaur called Prodinosaur. The dinosaur can fly and spawn Herobrine, and he is X-ray and can go through walls which is great. In the cave there was a dead end but Prodinosaur pressed a button and turned invisible. Someone went quickly past Prodinosaur and he started to run as fast as possible. The cave started to close but he got out safely and there was a spaceship. It opened up and it made a squeaking noise. It was black and orange. Then Prodinosaur was going off to Earth.

Alistair Mackay (9)
Hilton Of Cadboll Primary School, Tain

Sleeping In Flight

Axey was flying around but he was very tired and fell asleep in mid-air. He woke up to find two of his legs broken. He was hidden in a bush. A human was coming; Axey could tell because his one eye could see into the future. He tried to run but he wasn't used to walking on just two feet. He ran and ran and he went into a house, and hid under a bed until he recovered. A human child saw Axey as he spread his wings from his neck and flew off into the sunset.

Zachary Ray (9)
Hilton Of Cadboll Primary School, Tain

My Flaming Story

Flamo arrived at the School for Flames. He was in second class when the water alarm went off. They were all rushed outside. It was scary, everyone was outside, then the water people broke in and stole anything they found! Then Flamo ran into the school and kicked out the water people, and they left. Flamo got awarded school hero. The school day ended and Flamo loved school from now on!

William Whittaker (9)
Hilton Of Cadboll Primary School, Tain

Kawai-Puffball's Adventure

Once there was a cloud named Kawai-Puffball and she had magical powers that made her disappear every time someone tried to catch her. Kawai-Puffball had a pink fluffy body and she had super Kawai eyes that made people dizzy. She had so much fun making people dizzy. Kawai-Puffball had issues with her anger because people tried to catch her. She found a person named Ashley, Ashley was nice and she liked teaching Kawai-Puffball to be nice. Kawai-Puffball eventually became a kind puffball. Kawai and Ashley had the best time in the stranded school as they were going on the swings.

Charlotte Kidd (9)
Knockbreck Primary School, Tain

Bincey And Nancy-Pie's Adventure

On Friday, Bincey-Pie and Nancy-Pie went on an adventure to the baker's bin. Suddenly, Bincey-Pie found a mouldy piece of bread so he decided to eat it, but he didn't know it was magic. Soon he started to get bigger and bigger. He was usually blue but he was green now. 'What's wrong?' said Bincey-Pie. Then something weird happened, he started to shrink then he exploded. He was a tiny mince pie again but then he ate some more. This time he didn't grow, he shrank. Nancy-Pie was mad because he'd eaten more. She went red. Bincey-Pie said, 'Oopsy!'

Agnes Hooper (9)
Knockbreck Primary School, Tain

The Quest To Find Neptune

Major Sheepltin is the mayor of Sheepltin Town. During Boxing Day celebrations, he tried on his new rotating solar system hat when Neptune fell off. Now just to be clear, it is a very small fake Neptune, not the real one! Sheepltin searched high and low but it was not there. 'Where did it go?' wailed Sheepltin. Then he saw the wide, swinging, open door. 'Neptune must have rolled out of my room.' Meanwhile, Neptune had bounced down the stairs, *bong! Bong! Bong!* Sheepltin rushed down the huge stairs to find Neptune but Neptune was nowhere to be seen!

Eva Webster (9)
Knockbreck Primary School, Tain

Rastic-Red Rubber's Escape

It was April 1419, Rastic-Red Rubber was in a gloomy, dark classroom inside a pink pencil case, but Rastic-Red Rubber got out. Its thousand eyes jiggled when he flopped across the table then he came across some paper. It was stuck so Rastic-Red helped it into its big black paper box. When Rastic-Red Rubber turned back, he saw a big thick pencil and it did 360 degrees to trip Rastic-Red Rubber up, but Rastic-Red did a flip and ran away. He heard his family say, 'Hip, hip, hooray.' Rastic-Red climbed back into the pink pencil case with his rubbery family.

Rose Spriggs (10)
Knockbreck Primary School, Tain

No Homework

Five years ago, Bogtrot was walking on the street when she saw a school. She went in and looked for the homework and she found it! Now all she had to do was get it back to the borders of Lolland! She heard footsteps coming towards her... it was the teacher. Bogtrot shape-shifted into some paper but the teacher had seen her do it. Bogtrot shape-shifted back and ran, taking the homework! While she was running, the teacher gave up. Bogtrot took the homework inside her cave. 'Finally!' Bogtrot yelled. 'All the homework in Lolland! I am staying here forever!'

Niamh Jupp (9)
Knockbreck Primary School, Tain

Saveatron

On a Monday in 2018, Saveatron was building something in his workshop when he got a call from Santa. One of his reindeer had disappeared and Santa needed his help to find it. Saveatron was going to help but one of his rocket boosters didn't work. So Saveatron got a new booster and set off on his journey. It started to become cold so because he was made of metal, Saveatron started to freeze. He was almost there, he could see Santa's sleigh and the rest of the reindeer. But Rudolph wasn't there. Saveatron landed and helped Santa save Christmas.

Dominic Pumphery (9)
Knockbreck Primary School, Tain

The Different Dragon

As an egg slowly cracked, it revealed Sky, a cute little dragon with huge wings and a tail bigger than a classroom. Sky shot through the clouds, her huge wings right beside her and her tail wrapped around her like a skirt. Then it caught a breeze and she was in trouble. She straightened her wings out just before she hit the ground! She was in Dragondovia but there were no dragons anywhere. 'I know where they are,' said Bogtrot. 'They're in a land far away,' he continued. 'I'll give you them if you make it to the land Bogtea.'

Mackenzie Devaney (9)
Knockbreck Primary School, Tain

Durpy Mcturkey's Journey

When a man was killing turkeys, Durpy Mcturkey transformed into a mutant turkey to trick him into chasing him. The man started chasing Durpy Mcturkey into the water and Durpy Mcturkey transformed into his normal form. Durpy Mcturkey then took the man deep underwater. More men started coming to save the man and capture Durpy Mcturkey. Durpy Mcturkey started to go deeper and deeper but the men had caught up with him. They fought very badly against Durpy Mcturkey but he battled too well for them, so Durpy Mcturkey was victorious and took them back to land.

Jack Ross (9)
Knockbreck Primary School, Tain

Roger's Adventure!

As Roger started to climb the frosty mountain, it started to snow. He looked at the mountain. He had a long way to go. After thirty minutes, Roger heard a noise. He looked round the corner and he saw a dragon. They made friends and off they went to the top of the mountain. When they got there, they started to jump. After a while, Roger started to realise that he couldn't get to Mars by jumping, so they stopped. 'What am I going to do, little dragon?'

The dragon shrugged his shoulders. 'I don't know,' said the little dragon.

Liam Finlayson (9)
Knockbreck Primary School, Tain

Happy Mobile Does The Impossible

Thursday had come again. It was Running Over Day at Vehicle Army Camp. Happy Mobile was desperate to join and today he took his chance. He quietly sneaked past the snoozing security guard into the camp. Then Happy did the impossible stunt: up the ramp, through the ring of fire, and to top it off he ran over all the dummies. Happy held his breath. Had he done enough? Well, the leader did look quite impressed. So did the other members. The leader walked up to Happy and said, 'Sorry Happy, I guess we didn't know what you could do.'

Cuba Mamie Nicolson (9)

Knockbreck Primary School, Tain

Fangtom Fury

Long, long ago, far away, was a planet called Uranus. It was 1126 and there was a monster. It was called Fangtom. Fangtom lived in Fangty. After he had done his daily chores, he went to school. He used his grapple tongue to get to school. There was a spelling test. Fangtom was against Skadletron. Fangtom wanted to be the best at spelling but he got stuck. Fangtom used his toolkit tail to use the dictionary. When he found the word, his red horns shot out fire. But unfortunately he didn't know if he had beaten his enemy Skadletron...

Ramsay Rostock (9)

Knockbreck Primary School, Tain

Stocky-Stodo's Emerald

One day, a bad monster called Coal stole Stocky-Stodo's emerald, so Stocky-Stodo went on an adventure to find his emerald. Stocky-Stodo found a really hot forest so he shot ice cubes everywhere. Then it was nice and cold for him. When he finally got out of the forest happily, there was a wheat farm with a massive portal. Inside it was Coal. Stocky-Stodo shot an ice cube at Coal but he dodged it. Coal shot coal at Stocky-Stodo but he hit it with his wing. The coal hit the emerald out of Coal's hand. Stocky-Stodo went away.

Louie Macleod (8)
Knockbreck Primary School, Tain

The Flame And Water Battle

There was a Flame Knight called Fire-Death and his enemy was Water-Strike who was evil. Water-Strike has a water castle and the last time they met, Fire-Death managed to beat Water-Strike. After the battle, Fire-Death got home to his castle and was healed by the Healing Stone of Flames. Then he put on his helmet and gauntlets to get super powers. This would help him shoot out flames from his hands and beat Water-Strike once and for all. He would bring peace to the land, save all the Flame People, the king and the Fire Giants.

Will Russell (9)
Knockbreck Primary School, Tain

The Quest To Save Blobmas

On Blobmas Eve, before Blobmas, Bloby-D was going to the town hall in Bloby Town because he heard other blobs talking about something that happened to BlobyClaws recently. After Major Dob spoke, Bloby-D raced home to make a plan. When he was ready, he set off on his fun adventure. Soon he saw something red and gold, then he noticed it... it was the sleigh! He gasped in shock, then he saw a figure so he ran to the sleigh and saw BlobyClaws standing in the freezing cold. Bloby-D gave him a nice warm blanket and some warm milk.

Ellie Robb (9)
Knockbreck Primary School, Tain

The Unicorn Tale

Tom was walking in a dark forest and then he saw a beast drinking unicorn blood. The beast came to Tom and said, 'You look nice to eat. My name is Death-Bugs.' Tom pulled a gun out of his pocket and shot gum at the beast, and the gum hit Death-Bugs in the mouth. Tom laughed, Death-Bugs could not open his mouth. Tom locked Death-Bugs in a cell and then went home. Tom started to watch TV when he heard and saw a beast at the window. It was Death-Bugs! Tom walked outside with his gum machine to capture him.

George Hannah (9)
Knockbreck Primary School, Tain

The Potato Thief

In the Potato Kingdom, the Potato King saw a thief. He shouted, 'Stop!' then they ran out the kingdom, down the hill and into the shop. They were running around the shop until a terrifying shadow appeared. It was a human. The king got picked up and put in a bag. He ripped a hole in the bag and ran at the thief, back out the shop, up the hill and turned left. 'A car! Look out!' said the king. When the thief stopped, the king grabbed him and took him to the dungeon. Everyone lived happily ever after.

Kaan Baran (9)
Knockbreck Primary School, Tain

Slike's Adventure

Once upon a dimension in 2016, on Planet Hogmania, a creature called Slike was sad because all the monsters were scared of him. So he went on an adventure to get rid of his armour because it was turning him evil. He heard a noise. Looking at the slime he had made, he found the magic stick he was looking for. When he went to get it, jelly things came. Suddenly, the evil took over and turned him into a spike ball. As he pushed the jelly away, a stone landed on the stick, breaking off his extremely evil armour.

Riley Wilkinson (9)
Knockbreck Primary School, Tain

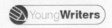

Big Adventure Of Bomb-Thrower

Long ago in Bomb Caven, December 7654, Bomb-Thrower was going home from his last adventure. As soon as he got in the house, he went to his room and he found a note saying 'Help!' He went to the mining cave. There was a puzzle, he had an idea in a snap. Behind the door was his family. Bomb-Thrower was about to set them free but he wasn't alone. Bomb-Thrower won with the finishing move, using his head. Bomb-Tricker gave him the key and then the family went home. Bomb-Tricker was defeated.

Shayne Thomas (9)
Knockbreck Primary School, Tain

62

The Stolen Pencil

On Monday, in a school playground, Mr Fizzy-Cola Bomb was looking for his best pencil. It was green and had black stripes. He remembered the humans had stolen it. So he ran into the school to look for it. Then a boy took it to write with. Mr Bomb started to panic in case he couldn't get it back. He would have to get it back when school finished. He sat there until he heard the bell ring. Then he sneaked back into class and got the pencil. He ran back to the forest but it was very, very dark.

Jack Mackie (8)
Knockbreck Primary School, Tain

The P5 Adventure

On the 2nd of December, on a planet far far away called Budy, in Scotton, Cotton-Dud was on a mission to plant the secret chip. He could slip through things because his blue body was so skinny. He slipped through the door and ran for his life. He just had to get the children on the floor, climb the electric wires then jump and get to the teacher to plant the chip in his ear. He snuck past children and he climbed up the wires. Cotton-Dud had to jump and put the chip in and he did it.

Lewis Alan Austin (9)
Knockbreck Primary School, Tain

Trielso Saves The Planet

Trielso was running, running fast. He was at Adventure Play, running away from Greany-Beeny who was chasing after him. 'I wish we could do this in real life,' said Greany-Beeny.

'Yeah,' said Trielso.

Suddenly, on the loudspeaker someone shouted, 'Alert! The whole planet is being disturbed. Go back to the pods now!'

'C'mon,' said Trielso, 'let's go.'

So they went back, but when they got back they found a human destroying their pod! At first they just stood there gawping but then finally Greany-Beeny shouted, 'Go!'

'Noooo!' said the human, then someone called...

'John, time for dinner!' and he left.

Iris-Mae Quilliam (9)

Riverside Primary School, Stirling

The Kindness Of Creatures

Stubby was sitting in his old wooden chair when he heard the post come through the mailbox. It was an invite to Pink PomPom's birthday party. 'I'm not going to that silly party,' he said. All of a sudden, there was a knock at the door.

'Hi,' said Jolly Mindset, 'are you coming to the party?'

'No,' said Stubby.

'But you have to come,' she said.

'Nooo!' he said.

'But there will be cake.'

'Noooo, I hate cake,' said Stubby.

'It's not very kind to get an invite and not go,' said Jolly Mindset.

'OK fine,' said Stubby, 'I'll go!'

Brooke Mirren Tait (9)
Riverside Primary School, Stirling

Flip Flop's Glow

Flip Flop is flapping his dark blue tail as fast as he can whilst getting chased by mermen. His long, extendable arm can get him far but not far enough; his only option is to hide. Flip Flop swims to the nearest cave and hides. Suddenly, he notices a mysterious green glow. 'Hello,' said a voice. 'Where am I?'

'You're in the Forbidden Cave. I will show you home,' it said.

'Okay,' Flip Flop said cautiously. The glow started to move. Flip Flop started to follow it. Slowly he began to see his home. 'Thank you.'

'It's fine.'

'Bye.'

'Bye.'

Sonny Williamson Frame (10)
Riverside Primary School, Stirling

Mushee And The Cat

One day, Mushee the mushroom was walking down the road when he heard the screaming of his friend, Mashee. 'What is wrong?' said Mushee.
'My cat is stuck up a tree.'
'Oh no,' said Mushee.
'Could you use your bouncing powers to save him?'
Mushee thought for a long hard while. 'Fine, I'll do it.' Mushee bounced as high as he could and grabbed the cat.
'Thank you so much,' said Mashee. The next day, Mushee went into town and met the mayor.
'This is a badge for bravery,' said the mayor.
'Thank you. I'm very happy about that!'

Stella Jamieson (9)
Riverside Primary School, Stirling

68

The Hobscotch Monster

'I know! Let's go looking for the Hobscotch!' Lucy suggested.

'Yes!' said Amelia. They jumped up and ran excitedly to the woods. Then they heard a peculiar sound. Suddenly, a giant slug jumped onto Amelia! 'Aaahhh!' she screamed.

'Hang on!' Lucy shouted. Lucy struggled to get it off, but when she did it disappeared into the ground. They continued on, then they heard another weird sound. It was the five-eyed giant stinky Hobscotch! 'Grrrrr!' it growled. They screamed and ran. He chased them through the woods and all the way home. But when they turned around he was gone!

Olivia Miller (9)
Riverside Primary School, Stirling

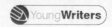

James And The Giant Walking Potato

James was walking past an old farmhouse. James saw a giant potato! James walked over to the potato, the potato stood and ran towards James! James screamed and ran away. The potato said, 'I am nice.'
James came back and said, 'Do you want to be friends?'
The potato said, 'Yeah, I have never had one.'
James and the potato went to the park. Everyone ran away because of the potato.
James said, 'Don't cry, they have probably never seen a walking potato!' James went to his house with Potato, they played Monopoly then James needed to go for dinner.

Jack Connelly (9)
Riverside Primary School, Stirling

Firelight And The Evil Snowball

Firelight was flying around Planet Snowdonia, trying to find some warm place to stay because her laser tail was losing its colour; she was too cold. She made herself invisible and snuck into someone's house. The house she went in was the Evil Snowball's! Firelight said to herself, 'At least Snowball can't see me.' But she still worried. Snowball was busy building his latest invention, the Snowball Shooter 3000. Then Firelight saw something glowing. She flew over to it, it was an energy cube. Just what she needed to get warm. Firelight recharged her tail, she was saved!

Phoebe Rose Saunders (9)
Riverside Primary School, Stirling

Mr Elli-fant

Once upon a time an Elli-fant was at the water hole minding his own business when suddenly... a mutant duck/chicken started to mock him, calling him an elephant, and everyone knows elephants are the enemy. The Elli-fant's name was Mr Elli-fant, he didn't have a first name. Mr Elli-fant ran away. Once he was away, he started to cry. 'I hate them, why do they mock me?' said Mr Elli-fant. 'Uh...' sighed Mr Elli-fant, 'I want to be normal.' Suddenly... there appeared a magic tiger that said, 'There's no such thing as normal or perfect.'

Jodie McDonald (11)
Riverside Primary School, Stirling

Return Of Bonkin!

Rapidly, Bonkin runs as fast as his tiny legs will go. Unfortunately, Bonkin has really small feet which don't allow much grip! But Bonkin does have very good eyesight with all of his six eyes! Amazingly, Rancohon, the Evil Lord, captured Bonkin but Bonkin isn't finished yet - he pulls out his six lightsabers and a battle commences! Rancohon is disadvantaged with only one lightsaber. Sadly for Bonkin, Rancohon has a full army of Rabindozz! Finally, Bonkin wins the battle and Rancohon breaks into two! Will Bonkin live forever or will he fall one day in the future?

Jonah Braccio Bracciali (9)
Riverside Primary School, Stirling

Yip's Missing Parents

Yip the Squardist was sad because he didn't know where his parents were. He went out flying with his big purple batwings to try and find them, his four legs streaming out behind him. His spotty, square tummy was rumbling because he was hungry for special Venus hot dogs. He flew to the supermarket to buy some. 'Do you have any special Venus hot dogs?' he asked.

'No,' the woman said. 'The last ones were bought by these two horned Squardists over there.' She pointed, Yip saw his parents. They had hot dogs together. Yip was happy he found them.

Elizabeth Newby (9)

Riverside Primary School, Stirling

Mission Rattle Snail

Spotty Dragon is sitting calmly on a bench, waiting for a mission. He's a dragon with two tails and big banana fingers, two antennae and a white body. Suddenly, his pocket bleeps. 'Yippee, a mission at last.' But what he doesn't know is he will face the dreaded...

Next thing he knows he is on the planet flying, his antennae and mouth big, and he meets his rival Rattle Snail. They start fighting immediately and soon Spotty Dragon nearly gets poisoned and heads back to base. The silly planet owner appoints Spotty Dragon head of the agency. Good has won!

Poppy-Ann Poole (10)

Riverside Primary School, Stirling

Cookie The Shape-Shifting Monster

'Hi, my name's Cookie and I'm a naughty shape-shifter. I live in China and I like playing pranks on certain people like my sister and her enemies. My first prank was on my sister, I shape-shifted into my sister's enemy and put clingfilm on her toilet seat!'

But Cookie got caught and was sent home when her sister saw the clingfilm. She ripped it off and tried to find Cookie who'd changed into someone else. Her sister called the police on her enemy and she went to jail. Cookie was about to tell her the truth but didn't say anything...

Summer Maclean (11)
Riverside Primary School, Stirling

The Adventure Of Mythical King Fluff Bomb

King Fluff Bomb bounced along happily on his adventure. Fluffy, galactical and up to mischief as usual he glanced at the giant towering building before him and decided to investigate. Inside was a huge trampoline surrounded by disco lights. He jumped on bouncing higher and higher until he completely lost his way and fell into an adjoining pit. Down, down, down he rolled until he arrived at the Land of Candy. Yummy candy! He thought this was the best day of his life until... he realised that Candy Land had been invaded by his enemies, the Fluff Snatchers!

Farah Waddell (9)
Riverside Primary School, Stirling

Silly, Sergeant Silly

Sergeant Silly is a naughty man who is the enemy of Just Jonathan and is up to more evil things. One day, Just Jonathan gets a phone call saying Sergeant Silly is going to destroy the planet of Plunco, where Jonathan is from! Sergeant Silly waits for Just Jonathan but he does not come, so Sergeant Silly says to himself, 'I'll wait a bit longer...'
Two years later, 'OK I'm ready, 3... 2... 1... fire!' But Sergeant Silly makes a big mistake and blows up his blimp, falls onto the electric surface of Plunco and dies because of the electricity!

Ollie Mawby (9)
Riverside Primary School, Stirling

The Hero Stone

Bob Brickly Scared is a cowardly monster from the planet Zog, and today is his least favourite day, Friday the 13th. Bob is so terrified of bricks that when he finds one he turns into liquid and slides away. Everyone laughs and shouts, 'Scaredy-cat, scaredy-cat!' That same day Bob went to Grandpa Brickly Scared's house and had a little wander about. He found a weird-looking object. It was something gold and shiny. Grandpa revealed it was an ancient hero stone which makes you scared of nothing. It was the stroke of twelve and Bob found another brick.

Lucy Abigail Cameron (8)
Riverside Primary School, Stirling

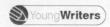

Time Hole Tragedy

Ploddy skipped along the beaten track until he stopped to take a breath, and then he saw it - a giant hole swirling around in the bushes. So Ploddy went to investigate but some sort of force sucked him in. 'Help!'
It suddenly went really dark and quiet until something grabbed him and a bright light shone down on him, and a voice said, 'Who are you?' Ploddy said, 'I'm Ploddy,' then he realised who was there. It was the Ferocious Pups, the creatures who had long tongues and lick you. Then Ploddy saw a door and ran...

Andrew Craig (9)
Riverside Primary School, Stirling

Adventure Of Creeps

Blobby leaves water torture causing five tsunamis already, but don't worry, he will freeze them. He starts sprinting and suddenly meets his enemies, Big Mouth and Diablo. Blobby sprints up to them with his mythical icy sword and suddenly stops. 'Hang on Big Mouth and Diablo, how about we be friends from now on?' Blobby, Big Mouth and Diablo shook hands and went on journeys together. The first one was when they went to capture an alien to prevent him falling in the volcano. It was almost too late, they ran to the volcano but it was too late.

Samuel Vargovsky (11)
Riverside Primary School, Stirling

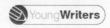

Vuducra Gets Lost

Vuducra stomped his way down the road on his bird-like feet. Vuducra started to get cold which was not usual for him. Usually he would be able to warm himself so he wouldn't faint. This wasn't normal. Vuducra noticed that there was nothing in his small town, he was freaked out. Vuducra tried to retrace his steps but couldn't get back. He saw a man, he walked over to him and asked for directions. The man said, 'Down the road and to the right.'
Vuducra said, 'That was so easy, can't wait to get to my hot, cosy home.'

Evan Ross Gillies (9)
Riverside Primary School, Stirling

The Fight Of Kerby And The King Of Pluto

As usual, Kerby was ruling Planet Wather. Everyone was enjoying their day because Kerby made it sunny and lots of aliens were at the beach. Soon it was morning again. It was mysterious, it was raining. Someone was coming, it was the king of Pluto. Kerby didn't like him. Everyone hid, Kerby made it thunder and lightning and hid in his house. *Bang!* on the door... Kerby came out and fought because he hated the king. *Boom! Bang!* The king of Pluto started to fight back then stopped because he came to be friends. Kerby said yes...

Kiara Steven (10)
Riverside Primary School, Stirling

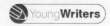

The Wardrobe

Bang! I woke up. It couldn't have been my dog, he doesn't make that much noise. I got out of bed and quietly but quickly opened my wardrobe. There was nothing there. I thought I was dreaming when something fluffy brushed past my bare leg. I jumped, I got the biggest fright of my life.
I went to school but couldn't stop thinking about what happened so I told my friends. They didn't believe me so they came over to my house after school. When we got there we saw a small, purple, fluffy monster playing with my dog Snow!

Jennifer Raiston (9)
Riverside Primary School, Stirling

The Adventures Of Mr Purple Butt

Some time ago there was a creature called Mr Purple Butt. He lived on Pluto Under Fish but all the fish were mean to him. When he was sad he changed colour. One day, he was so sad he changed from purple to blue, green, yellow, orange and red! He turned rainbow next. People on Pluto Under Fish called this rainbow fish a god, but when he was happy he turned back to purple. When everyone was mean again Mr Purple Butt said, 'We're all fish and family, so we should never be mean to each other.'

'Yay!' shouted everyone.

Robyn Elizabeth Harley (9)
Riverside Primary School, Stirling

Miss Bobblybee Lost In Space

Miss Bobblybee is a friendly alien, she has eight eyes and a sausage-like body. She lives on Planet Jupiter, and one day her enemy, Sprick, who lived next door, put noise putty on her doorstep. When Miss Bobblybee was leaving to go to her friend's house, she stepped right into the pile of putty which made an enormous bang! She was so annoyed she just went back to bed and didn't go to her friend's. Then Sprick had a think and went to Miss Bobblybee's house, and said sorry for the problem. Then they became best friends forever!

Lillian Baxter (9)

Riverside Primary School, Stirling

The Cute Bunny Den

Once upon a time a cute bunny named Cutey lived in a small stick den in Mine Woods in Bridge Of Allan. He started building his den after he turned eleven years old. He had spent two years building the small den where he lived. Later on one day he finished building. A big, enormous rabbit came into his den and said, 'Hello Son.'

Cutey froze in shock. Cutey then said 'Hello Father! How are you doing?'

His father said 'I am very well thank you.' All of a sudden, the wind managed to blow Cutey's house over!

Conal Doherty (11)
Riverside Primary School, Stirling

Battle Of The Leader

Once upon a time there was a leader and that leader was Galoobob. One morning, he sent his worker to get some wood. 'Come see this, Galoobob,' said a soldier.

'OK,' said Galoobob. So he set out to find out about what the soldier said. 'I've found a village,' said Galoobob, suddenly from a glimpse from his eye he saw something blue. It was very fast. It stopped and walked over to Galoobob. He offered Galoobob a gift but he said no and tried to fire poison at him. Galoobob hit him and they killed each other!

Joe Underwood (10)
Riverside Primary School, Stirling

Best Friendship

Once there were three friends called Giggley, Spiky and Facey. Giggley always giggled, that's why he was Giggley. Spiky had spikes all over his body and Facey had two faces. One day, Giggley's 9th birthday party came. He invited Spiky, Facey and his other friends. Spiky gave Giggley an ice cream maker, Facey gave him Star Wars toys. After a while, they started fighting about whose gift was the best. Giggley tried to sort it out and he said to them, 'Both your gifts were really good.' Then they all lived happily ever after.

Rushmail Afzal (9)
Riverside Primary School, Stirling

Uh-Oh, This Isn't Right

When Zamelya plonked out of the building, all she could see was green and orange. As she walked around, she suddenly felt alarmed because she was in the Ice King's home town. In the distance she saw a castle, *That's the Ice King's castle*, she thought. She arrived with a cracked horn. She saw the Ice King pacing about, Zamelya jumped out and shot the Ice King with magic but it deflected and hit the wall. She did it again and the Ice King fell to the ground. Zamelya got back to Planet Unicorn and lived there forever.

Eva Willow Coulter (8)
Riverside Primary School, Stirling

Can't Eat?

There was a creature called Sligoo, he was very slimy and green. Sligoo had five eyes, lots of tentacles, and his fangs were as sharp as sharks' teeth. He was also stinky.

It's one o'clock, Sligoo finds a school! Looking for some food, he sees something but it is too hairy. Now he finds the right thing, a fish. He looks around, no one's in the classroom. He eats the fish but doesn't feel like he has it in his tummy. Sligoo sees the fish on the floor. Oh no, it slips through his body! Have you ever seen that?

Anna Maria Blazejczyk (9)
Riverside Primary School, Stirling

Mars Takeover

Once upon a time, there was a creature called ZeeZee who lived on Planet Mars. Mars was a peaceful, happy planet. ZeeZee was the leader and all of the planet adored her.

One sunny day, Zuky came to Mars to take leadership. ZeeZee and her planet did not like Zuky as he was nasty and mean. Zuky tried to form an army to fight against ZeeZee but the creatures of the planet would not side with Zuky.

Zuky eventually gave up and ZeeZee was leader once again. Then they all made up and Mars was peaceful and happy once again.

Sophie Mulvenna (9)
Riverside Primary School, Stirling

Merlana's New Home

Merlana had been told a horrible thing. She had to leave her home city of Anchovia because it was fishing season and the mad fishermen had nearly captured half of Oceanopolis. She sadly waved goodbye to her underwater friends. Now Merlana had to fly to Cloud Kingdom, a land in the clouds she usually went on her holiday to. When she landed on Cloud Kingdom, she thought about her home and how she would never get to swim any more. Then she saw a hole in her tail, it got bigger and inside were feet. 'I can walk!' she cried.

Rhona Joanne Waldron (9)

Riverside Primary School, Stirling

Soria Sunton The Flying Gymnast

Soria Sunton was alone wandering, then she decided that she would go on a walk. As she got up from Sulby Bay, her pinkish-black hair was flowing, her four tentacles swaying and her big feet stamping. Later she did not know where she was. She got lost and the next thing she knew, she had met her arch-enemy, Niokia Nerd, at Monstrous Mountain. 'I will show you the way back if you tell me the code of Face Lava,' she said. Soria cartwheeled over Niokia's head, then over a bridge and then she was home. Hip, hip, hooray!

Hekaya Makafui Esi Ry-Kottoh (10)
Riverside Primary School, Stirling

Wecome Home, Boby!

There was a little green alien called Boby. His planet was being invaded by humans. Just in time a dark figure pulled him into a rocket and they blasted off into the dark starry sky. When they landed Boby was left on a new planet all alone. He walked along a cold pathway on a dark smoky planet. Someone jumped out and chased him. He ran as fast as he could around a corner and bashed into two familiar faces. 'We are your parents, Boby, and you're coming home because everything's safe. Welcome home, Boby!'

Lyla Campbell (10)
Riverside Primary School, Stirling

The Adventures Of Bog-Zog

Bog-Zog is surrounded by monsters from other planets called Dizorm, Big-Bob and Sun-Hut. The monsters are Bizorm, Lottia and Zomiy. Bizorm has fire powers, Lottia has ice powers and Zomiy has invisibility powers. They help Bog-Zog get the Zog stone. On the quest they pass Dizorm, Big-Bob and Sun-Hut. Finally they get to the end of Zog and try to find the Zog stone and they do. When they get to Zog they give the stone to the emperor of Zog. He is so pleased he makes Bog-Zog the new emperor of the planet Zog.

Nicole Elise Schiavone (9)
Riverside Primary School, Stirling

When The Piano Attacks

Obsornortute was just walking along when he got sucked up by a portal which took him to Human Land. Obso had a scary journey to Human Land (Earth) before plodding along, shooting his guns at passers-by. Then Obso reached a really big market where they sold Obso's enemy: pianos. Obso got angry at the pianos and shot his lasers and guns at them. Then, out of nowhere, the pianos started moving and attacking Obso. Obso was now so angry that he shouted out that he made the wrong decision to come to this strange planet!

James Anderson Taylor (9)
Riverside Primary School, Stirling

The Story Of El Diablo

El Diablo is a Volcano-Head Beast that lives in Fiery Pit. He also has a bite on his body, he got it from fighting Hellhounds. He has his companion, Carl the Cookie. El Diablo (Diablo for short) wanted to escape Fiery Pit, so he ran to the gates then said, 'I thought the gates would be locked.' Then Diablo saw a golden staircase, he walked up. He saw daylight and water cannons. He tired to run, the guards caught him. They started shooting at him and he got smaller, but suddenly he started to get bigger...

Brian Duguid (11)
Riverside Primary School, Stirling

Elliet The Stink King!

Elliet the very clumsy alien, with yellow pencil legs, red crab claws, green tentacles and a green body, had his first day of school. When he got home, tears ran down his face from one big eye. From then on, every day he came home crying. He was getting bullied by older children.

One day he came home and discovered that he had the power of stink, he wasn't sure how though. He used this against his enemies and scared them away. Elliet found a new friend the same age as him. His name was so cool, it was Ross.

Rebecca Menzies (9)
Riverside Primary School, Stirling

Lost

Uni woke up with a start. She didn't know where she was. In her country, Hornland, it was warm not cold. She walked around and there was nothing but snow. Uni found a boat, it was very old-looking. There was a map, she spotted her country on the map. It took seven days to get home. She had to walk from the beach to her home. She found her mum, dad, seven brothers and two sisters. She was so happy to be home and safe in Hornland after all. She lived happily ever after in her lovely little house.

Maya Templeton (8)

Riverside Primary School, Stirling

Football Superstar

Slobbybob was getting ready for a match. When he was ready he set off and met his team-mates and waited for the match to start. He said to one of his team-mates, 'I hope Bad Guy isn't playing on the other team,' but it was too late, he was playing on the other team.

At the end of the match, Bad Guy's team were playing really well and they won. The score was 3-2 to Bad Guy's team. Slobbybob's team did make up for it but Bad Guy and his team said, 'We will win again next time.'

Callum Stephen James Dewar (10)

Riverside Primary School, Stirling

Mickwin Has Returned

It was a dark, stormy night and when Mickwin woke up in the morning, he was not at his island. He was in a dungeon cell. No way was Mickwin going to spend the rest of his life in a cell. So two days later, Micklose has a meeting at the Slimepop's and when Micklose is at his meeting, Mickwin will use his plan of action. The plan is to get flushed down the toilet and escape through the sewers. It's time to escape through the sewer. When Mickwin got home, his house was gone! Mickwin sat down and thought...

Zachary Ferguson (9)
Riverside Primary School, Stirling

Speed Is Key!

It was a stormy night, Sonic was running against his rival, Shadow. He spread his lasers, he had to run and make Shadow dizzy. Suddenly, the ground started to shake, lasers were fired but it wasn't Shadow... That meant it was Galoobob! One of the lasers hit Shadow, luckily Galoobob fell down the mountain. Sonic sprinted to try to catch Shadow but it was too late. Sonic had a tear in his eye. Sonic ran up the hill and sliced Galoobob with his sword, and at the same time a laser hit Sonic! He was so dead.

Lewis David Paterson (10)

Riverside Primary School, Stirling

Untitled

Bloby, the green slimy monster, was making a meal for his wife and children when there was a knock at the door. Bloby went to open the door but didn't realise that it was Black Fur. So he opened the door, straight away Black Fur drew his sword. Bloby shouted to his wife and children to hide. Then he started to wrap his top eyes around Black Fur. After that, Bloby shot poison into him and he fell to the floor dead. He called his wife and children and said it was safe, and they lived happily ever after.

Emily Collington (10)
Riverside Primary School, Stirling

Bad To Good

A bright, colourful creature was walking in the dungeon maze with three eyes and six blue arms. He was called Spot the Healer! He was walking and walking, trying to get out, suddenly he saw a *massive* green mess. Spot knew it was Mr Colp (Mr Colp is Spot the Healer's worst enemy). Spot tried to tell Mr Colp not to hurt him and that they could work together. Mr Colp stopped and said that he wanted to team up as well. They teamed up and they tried to get out. After one hour they finally got out.

Sophie O'Sullivan (9)

Riverside Primary School, Stirling

Zorg's Fright

Zorg was feeling sad and lonely as he walked back home. He lived on Planet Zor, he was small, blue and fluffy with a big mouth and scary teeth. Today he was feeling sad because he was all alone. As he walked he saw a big, dark shadow moving slowly in front of him... the shadow turned creepily to look at him and Zorg froze with fright. Luckily, he was a shape-shifter so he turned into a log to hide himself. It turned out to be his friend, Lorg. Zorg was really happy and transformed himself back into a Zor.

Thomas Edmiston (9)
Riverside Primary School, Stirling

The Folfs And Me

My name is Alexandra and I am a Folf. There are only twenty of my kind. We are happy here in Canada but our migration is today! OMG, I'm so excited! We get to run across Lake Toha, maybe the tourists will take pictures! I'll comb my hair just in case! I get to run on my own this year since I'm thirteen! See, we Folfs have special powers, like walking on water and jumping really high like the house cats that you humans have as pets. Well, my mother is howling for me, talk to you later. Bye-bye!

Gwen McAviney (11)

Riverside Primary School, Stirling

Max And The Rocket Car

Max flew in a rocket to his rocket mill for flour, suddenly his eyes saw a strange car. Max thought, *if I fix it I will have the car...* 'A rocket car!' yelled Max. 'What's better: a car or a rocket? Hmm...' Max got into the car and saw the red button. He pressed it and the car started off with crazy speed! Max pressed the button again but the car didn't slow... Suddenly, Max woke up. 'It looks like everything I dreamed!' said Max. What a wonderful adventure!

Mikolaj Jasinski (9)
Riverside Primary School, Stirling

The Cake Has Been Swiped!

Stalategg skipped along the bumpy surface of the planet Heka Deka Peka. With her white egg body, her black Cyclops eye in a crack in the egg body, her elephant trunk mouths, tentacles, patterned skirt, blue boots and curly hair, she looked a sight! As she skipped along the purple grass, she had an ache of hunger. She made a grab for her pocket, her cake was gone! She turned and saw the Sticky Pad Stick Monster sprint off with it! She growled and chased after him. She was gonna get her cake back!

Nuala Scully (10)
Riverside Primary School, Stirling

Short Sam And A Smelly Shock!

Short Sam was a short smelly alien that loved fighting. He always said to all of the aliens that they are dumb, then he would go invisible so they could not punch Short Sam. He always loved to shower in poo and people thought he was bad and did not like him. One day a massive monster came to Short Sam and said, 'Do you want to fight?' Sam said yes, but before it started Sam could smell poo. The monster was wearing poo. He said to Sam, 'You're not the only one that can!'

Callum Draper (9)

Riverside Primary School, Stirling

Bloby's Big Day Out

Bloby was a silly alien from Mars, he had three rainbow eyes and his skin was orange and slimy. He had no legs and slithered around on his butt. His most amazing talent was that he could change shape! Bloby was slithering down the street when he fell down a drain but being his own slithery self he thought, *What if I change shape to escape?* He turned into a bird and flew out of the drain. He flew up into the sky and met Bobena, and they lived happily ever after in their bloby house.

Abbie Coutts (8)
Riverside Primary School, Stirling

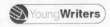
A Bird From Mars

It was a dark night and Ewulf was lying on a bed of hay with the gentle wind blowing his red and grey fur. He was chewing a dead bird that a fox had dropped the night before. Through the shattered window of the house he could hear a screeching noise carried by the wind. He moved towards the window and transformed into a small bird. He flew through the window, landed and turned back into a wolf. A bird was in the tree, it had the body of an eagle and the head of a duck called Duckle...

Ezra Jump (11)
Riverside Primary School, Stirling

The Solid Monster

My monster is a very bad monster because he's scary and shouts at people. I got a scare as well, he is a very ugly and sinister-looking monster. When he went to prison he was a very angry monster and attacked the guard. He pushed through everyone and unfortunately got out. But then a big, tough guard came and threw him into another jail cell. The monster got really mad and ended up banging his head on the wall, and his body was moving very slowly before he fell unconscious.

Lewis John Reid (11)
Riverside Primary School, Stirling

Fire At School!

Once upon a time there was a monster called Firey. He woke up with a jump that went up from his foot! Firey went to school and in class his tongue was burning-hot. He discovered he had a power, a fire tongue! The next thing that came to his head was that he should be a super villain. So he secretly set his classroom on fire! The fire alarm went off. Firey started setting the entire school on fire! Firey was sent to the police station and was put in jail for 100 years.

Evan Rands (9)
Riverside Primary School, Stirling

The Head Eater

A blue and purple hovering monster with five eyes was going down the street. Then a buzzer buzzed and he went zooming off (I think his name was Hover Horn). He ended up at a school that was being attacked by Mr Frog. He was biting all the teachers' heads off! Hover Horn got his Head Zapinator out and put all the heads back on the teachers. He threw Mr Frog in jail and made his way back to Planet Fogles. Hover Horn had a very happy life after this!

Holly Matheson (10)
Riverside Primary School, Stirling

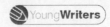

The Stubby Palm Tree

A stubby little palm tree flew from his home to a region warm and tropical. He sat on a sandy beach and then day by day he got taller each day but didn't know he was growing taller. He walked to the beach and then he looked at something behind him. He noticed a tail with a face and he tried to wiggle it about but it didn't work. The head popped out and gave the palm tree a scare. The stubby palm tree was no longer stubby!

Connor Iain James Cadger (10)
Riverside Primary School, Stirling

Dragon Vile Mess Up

Glong Spagle squelched along on the streets of Dragon Vile and shape-shifted into a dragon, going to an acrobatic competition. But someone was watching him. When Glong Spagle got to the competition it was his turn. He flipped onto the poles easily, but a dragon scared Glong Spagle and he turned into a ball and bounced through the course. Done!

Alex Harrower (9)
Riverside Primary School, Stirling

The Adventure

Spiko Dude stomped through the muddy puddle and hopped stone to stone to avoid the lava. He teleported to meet Stitchy. 'Oh no, I'm on Earth, that means I'm stuck.' Suddenly, something bumped into Spiko Dude.
'Are you an alien from outer space?'
'How do you know?'
'I love reading books about aliens. Do you need help getting home?'
'If you don't mind.'
'Sure. How many times have you teleported?'
'About a hundred.'
'Wow, you need to change what you do to teleport.'
'OK, I can stomp three times, I'll try that.'
It worked, finally Spiko Dude was home.

Anna Brown (9)
Stanley Primary School, Perth

The Capture!

One day, J.J.Jim was with his dad on Mars, then the Whipes came and stole him. J.J.Jim used his laser eyes and stunned one of them in their massive ship. But there was still no hope. J.J.Jim started to cry when a Cookie Man (the mayor of Mars) arrived, lashing at the air fiercely. J.J.Jim ran away home to his mum. His mum said, 'Why are you crying?'

'Dad has been captured by the Whipes!' he said in a muffled voice.

'Then we'll get them and destroy their ship as well,' said Mum. 'They deserve it the way they are.'

Edward Trevallion (9)
Stanley Primary School, Perth

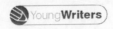

Untitled

One day, Blobby Splat was riding to the skate park. Fuzz Wuzz showed up and said, 'You want to ride?' Blobby Splat thought that was good because Fuzz Wuzz was usually his enemy. So they rode together. They played a game of bikes. After that, Fuzz Wuzz pushed Blobby Splat, Blobby Splat punched him back. One week later, Blobby Splat finally made a friend who was a biker. His friend was called Reven, he saw a fight, a real fight. Blobby Splat and Reven were friends for ages and ages, they would go about NYC on their bikes!

Josh Jerome (10)
Stanley Primary School, Perth

Bobby Low

Bobby Low lives in a dark, dusty, misty cave. He is four years old on the planet Guava Juice. He stomped through the windy forest until unexpectedly, a fluffy soft sheep appeared. The sheep seemed scared for his life. He mistook Bobby for a scary, angry monster. Bobby was sad but on the scary walk home, Bobby saw the sheep and shouted, 'Hi, I'm a friendly monster, not a mean monster.' Bobby Low and the sheep became best friends forever and took walks together and played all day long. Such a happy ending.

Cara Lee (10)
Stanley Primary School, Perth

The Adventures Of Rainbow Star

On a summer morning, with the scent of daisies in the air, me and my sister RainbowSplash were going to the park. We were playing on the climbing frame and RainbowSplash fell. She screamed in agony, she was petrified. She had to go to the hospital, she got an X-ray and we found out that she didn't break her leg. So we went home and had hot chocolate. Then Granny came and visited us for an hour then we went to bed. Granny was reading us stories. I could not get to sleep so RainbowSplash and I played doctors.

Olivia Keenan (9)
Stanley Primary School, Perth

The Move

Gorg Horns the Eno was in a sphere spaceship disguised as a planet. They were going to another planet called Earth. They took all the humans out of their home to Australia where no Enos were. Gorg Horns settled into his new home. Gorg Horns decided to explore the place outside, he was on his way to the woods when he met a girl called Pip who was thirteen. Gorg Horns was a welcoming and gentle Eno so he didn't hurt her. Pip was a pretty and clever girl, and she wasn't afraid of him. They became friends.

Dreanna Norris (10)
Stanley Primary School, Perth

Rainbow Fluffy Fluff Land

One fluffy sunny day there was a cute fluffy monster, he was called Rainbowchue. He was playing with Spikodude, his BFF. They enjoyed playing Rainbow Tig, this is when they used their amazing magical powers. They were having such fun but suddenly they fell in a weird dark hole with a few pieces of wood. They magically made a ladder. They got up, they could smell strawberries - they were in the wrong land. They tried to find the way, Rainbowchue suddenly teleported to Rainbow Fluffy Fluff Land.

Ethan Sam Low (9)
Stanley Primary School, Perth

Adventure In Candy Land

One day, DJ Zoe woke up in her little house, got dressed and went outside to find herself not in Troll Land but in Candy Land. The trees were candy canes, the ground was made of peppermints. So she decided to go for a walk when she heard a massive squelch. It felt like she had stood in something. She was frozen, she couldn't move no matter what. When she looked down she realised she'd stepped in a great big puddle of Quick Mint. She used her disc power to cut herself free and ran home.

Daisy Morgan (9)
Stanley Primary School, Perth

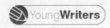

Untitled

The monster's name is Eaglesache. He came from the sun. He's spotty and he has got really sharp fangs. He can jump really high, he can turn into stuff. He is strong, his skin can camouflage and when he evolves his skin comes off! He gets wings only when he eats lava rocks and drinks lava. He will drink all the lava in the volcano and destroy the world, and it will be the end of the world! The people of Sholgers can kill it but he is too strong, he will kill everyone...

Dillon Williamson (9)
Stanley Primary School, Perth

The Rainbow Sisters

On a warm, sunny day, a breeze carried the fresh scent of flowers to Rainbow Splash. She was at the park with her big sister, Rainbow Star. She was desperate to copy Rainbow Star because she was so cool. Rainbow Splash started to climb after her sister but the climbing frame was slippy and *swoosh!* Rainbow Splash fell and thought she had broken her leg. She had to go to the hospital, she was in that much agony that she got an X-ray but her leg was not broken.

Courtney Nicoll (10)
Stanley Primary School, Perth

Backflip Bob

In the morning, Bob Junior woke up and put his padding on to protect him from the sun. After that, he stomped on his massive feet and slid along the face of the sun and powered up his jetpack. He bellowed, 'Jetpack away!' and pressed 'Full Power'. When he got to Planet Earth, his jetpack broke and he fell on a trampoline, did a double backflip, landed on a roof and climbed into a chimney. Then he shot back up to the sun.

Alex Russell (9)
Stanley Primary School, Perth

Going To Earth To Make Friends

Mistacha left his house to go to school. There was a rocket outside, he took the rocket to go to Earth. He landed and trembled to the park and all the children sprinted home. Mistacha cried because everyone was afraid of him. Two children returned. Mistacha told them, 'I don't have any friends.'
'We will be your friends.'
Mistacha travelled home to Pluto and promised he would visit them every week.

Ryan Andrew (9)
Stanley Primary School, Perth

Dragonfly And Dragon School

One day, there was a little egg coloured orange and white. It was lost in the Amazon rainforest. The little egg was hatching, *ccrack!* Oh look, it's a dragonfly, how cute. Suddenly, three hunters came along. 'Oh look, a dragonfly, how much could we sell that for?'

'Around 100 pounds.'

Suddenly, out of nowhere, Dragonfly made lightning come down on the hunters. Then a brave man called Bob appeared, Bob the Fighter. Bob said to Dragonfly, 'Look at you, let's take you to my house. You can go to Dragon School. You will learn to control your power there.'

Jack Stephen (9)
Tulloch Primary School, Perth

Werevamp

Werevamp is a werewolf vampire who lives in Monsterburg on Monster Island. He has pointy fangs, shorts, a black hat, claws, red eyes, lots of hair and bloodstained teeth. One night, Werevamp went to Wales to get some blood but as he got to a house, he heard a noise. 'Who's there?' he said. Suddenly, a very tall man appeared with garlic. 'Aahhh!' Werevamp cried. He ran to the docks, jumped into a boat and sped away. Later that night, Werevamp sat up in bed. 'I hate tall men!' he said and fell asleep.

McKenzie William Yeaman (10)
Tulloch Primary School, Perth

The Three-Legged Wolf

One day, I was meeting Grace in the woods. It was going to be fun, we were looking for Max the three-legged wolf! I texted Grace as it was now dark and asked her to meet me at the wooden gate. As I waited, I saw a twinkling flash of lights. *Is it Max's eyes?* I thought. My heart was pounding fast. Where was Grace? She should've been here by now. Max approached me, sat, stared and howled. I noticed a necklace around one of his necks. One that Grace always wore. Could the wolf be Grace? I froze!

Hannah McGregor (9)
Tulloch Primary School, Perth

The Monster Invasion

A long time ago, in a galaxy far far away, there were monsters in their world. Today we will be talking about a dragon called Bog. Bog was a cheeky dragon. Bog was going home, when he got back to Mars he saw people trapped in cages. Bog was not happy! *Who's doing this?* thought Bog. *Maybe Crazydude?* Bog and Crazydude hated each other. Crazydude had blue laser eyes, a million wings, twenty legs and was pure evil. He lived on Jupiter. Was it Crazydude who had trapped all these people?

Charlie Swan (9)
Tulloch Primary School, Perth

The End Of The World

One morning, me and my friends Lucy and Jeff went on an adventure in the woods. All we heard was groaning and growling. So we crept on to investigate the noises we were hearing, suddenly Jeff stopped so we went over to see why he had stopped. It was Doctor Stretch! We quickly ran to my house to get a hose because he was very slimy. We went back to the woods so we could destroy Doctor Stretch! We climbed up trees so he didn't see us, then we fired a shot and he was dead so we celebrated.

Blair Michael Rogalski (8)
Tulloch Primary School, Perth

Sloggy The Crazy Creature

There was this monster named Sloggy, his home planet was Zogger and his parents loved him very much. Then they died. Sloggy was very sad but then he said, 'I will gain super powers for my parents so they will love me as spirits. I know they will.' So he tried experiments. On his 100th attempt he did it right and got super powers. After that he tried to make his parents live again and it worked! Sloggy was so happy that he cried and they all lived happily ever after.

Philip Kubelka (8)
Tulloch Primary School, Perth

The Adventure Of Creepy Five And Flying Horse

One night, CreepyFive and FlyingHorse were flying around the sky then they saw Goatman, an evil villain, breaking into a bank. CreepyFive and FlyingHorse landed at the back of the bank, CreepyFive knew a secret entrance into the bank. They hid whilst Goatman made his way towards them and CreepyFive pounced on Goatman, and wrapped his alien hands around him whilst FlyingHorse breathed fire over Goatman. That was that, the end of Goatman. He was exterminated for good!

Grace Ashforth (8)
Tulloch Primary School, Perth

The Battle On The Sun

I was in a big battle on the sun and my wings got set alight in massive flames. Big holes started to appear in my wings and I got deep, large scars on my chest and arms. Suddenly, I got sucked into a massive black hole that sent me into space. Eventually, I woke up on another planet called Jupiter and I saw a monster that was taller than me. I tried to fly away but my holed burnt-out wings stopped me. I started to run away and that was the end of my life.

Jack Dermot Hennessy (8)
Tulloch Primary School, Perth

Fireboy

One day, Fireboy saw Waterman turn people into rocks. Fireboy went to Waterman and he told Waterman to stop turning people into rock.
Waterman said, 'No!'
Fireboy said, 'I'm going to be angry if you don't stop!'
Waterman looked and shouted, 'No!' again! So Fireboy ran and used his fire power and turned him into rock too.

Titan Miller (9)
Tulloch Primary School, Perth

YoungWriters
Est.1991

YOUNG WRITERS INFORMATION

We hope you have enjoyed reading this book – and that you will continue to in the coming years.

If you're a young writer who enjoys reading and creative writing, or the parent of an enthusiastic poet or story writer, do visit our website **www.youngwriters.co.uk**. Here you will find free competitions, workshops and games, as well as recommended reads, a poetry glossary and our blog.

If you would like to order further copies of this book, or any of our other titles, then please give us a call or visit **www.youngwriters.co.uk**.

Young Writers
Remus House
Coltsfoot Drive
Peterborough
PE2 9BF
(01733) 890066
info@youngwriters.co.uk